The Frightened Frog

First published in 2010
by Wayland

Text copyright © Joe Hackett
Illustration copyright © Mike Spoor

Wayland
338 Euston Road
London NW1 3BH

Wayland Australia
Level 17/207 Kent Street
Sydney, NSW 2000

Editor: Katie Powell
Series Editor: Louise John
Cover design: Paul Cherrill
Design: D.R.ink
Consultant: Shirley Bickler

A CIP catalogue record for this book is available from the British Library.

ISBN 9780750260039

Printed in China

Wayland is a division of Hachette Children's Books,
an Hachette UK Company

www.hachette.co.uk

The Frightened Frog

Written by Joe Hackett
Illustrated by Mike Spoor

WAYLAND

e sho
n be
owers
hone
ode
can
ew o
cha
ed i
rge

The class were going on a school trip to the countryside. All the animals stood waiting for the bus, chatting together.

Everyone except for Finlay the frog. He waited by himself, hopping up and down, looking anxious.

"Come on, Finlay. Get on the bus," called Mrs Hooper, the teacher. "We're going to a big lake. You'll be able to swim as much as you want."

"I don't like swimming," grumbled Finlay, climbing on board.

"Don't be silly! All frogs like swimming," said Mrs Hooper.

When the bus arrived at the countryside, Finlay looked out of the window. There were trees and fields as far as the eye could see. And a lovely clear blue lake!

Finlay sat on his seat, looking very upset.

"What's wrong, Finlay?" grunted Patty the pig.

"It's the lake!" wailed Finlay.

"The lake looks lovely! I expect you'll jump straight in," said Toby the terrier.

"No I won't!" mumbled Finlay, as the class got off the bus. "I'm not very good at swimming."

"Why ever not?" asked Latif the lion.

"I had hundreds of brothers and sisters and they all grew faster than me," sniffed Finlay. "I was the last one to learn to swim. To tell you the truth, I'm a bit frightened of the water."

"But you're a frog! All frogs like water. Birds don't worry about flying," said Oliver the owl. "Watch me!"

Oliver soared up into the air.

"Flying is fun," he hooted. "I can even do tricks!"

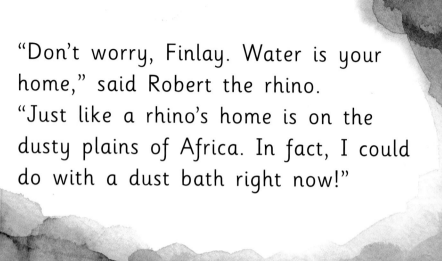

"Don't worry, Finlay. Water is your home," said Robert the rhino.
"Just like a rhino's home is on the dusty plains of Africa. In fact, I could do with a dust bath right now!"

Robert began to roll about in the earth.
He sent clouds of dust into the air,
covering the other animals.

Mrs Hooper spotted Robert making
a mess.

"That's enough, Robert!" she boomed.

Robert stopped immediately. "Sorry,
Mrs Hooper. I was only trying to cheer
Finlay up," he said.

"What's the matter, Finlay?" asked
Mrs Hooper.

"Everyone wants me to swim, but I'm
not very good at it," Finlay sniffed.

"I'm sure that's not true," said Mrs Hooper, kindly. "Come on, let's go to the lake."

Finlay crouched on the edge of the lake but he still refused to go in.

"I know!" said Mrs Hooper. "Let me show you how to swim."

All the animals sat quietly on the bank. Some of them were thinking that Mrs Hooper was the wrong shape to swim — too big and fat.

But Mrs Hooper swam very well for such a large animal. She kept her nose out of the water and she kicked her feet one at a time.

In fact, Mrs Hooper looked right at home!

"This is the way to do it, Finlay,"
Mrs Hooper called.

"Oh, no! Frogs don't swim like that," Finlay croaked. "We kick both legs together at the same time and go much faster!"

"Well, why don't you show us then?" encouraged Mrs Hooper.

"Yes, come on, Finlay," said Latif
the lion.

Finlay hopped to the edge of the lake
and crept into the water. It felt cool
in the summer sunshine.

"Ooh, the water feels lovely," said Finlay, looking surprised.

Carefully, Finlay pushed out into the middle of the lake.

"This is the way we swim," said Finlay, a bit nervously.

Then, kicking both his webbed back feet at the same time, Finlay shot across the lake.

"Look at me!" said Finlay.
"I'm swimming!"

Then, just to show how good he was, Finlay climbed out of the water and dived back in head first.

SPLASH!

"We knew you could do it!" cheered the other animals, clapping their hands. "Well done, Finlay!"

START READING is a series of highly enjoyable books for beginner readers. **The books have been carefully graded to match the Book Bands widely used in schools.** This enables readers to be sure they choose books that match their own reading ability.

Look out for the Band colour on the book in our Start Reading logo.

The Bands are:

Pink Band 1A & 1B

Red Band 2

Yellow Band 3

Blue Band 4

Green Band 5

Orange Band 6

Turquoise Band 7

Purple Band 8

Gold Band 9

START READING books can be read independently or shared with an adult. They promote the enjoyment of reading through satisfying stories supported by fun illustrations.

Joe Hackett was born on a farm. He remembers riding on a horse so big that he couldn't get his legs across its back. Now he lives on a little farm again, with his wife and dog Ozzie, who is small, black and brown, and loves best of all to go down badger and rabbit holes.

Mike Spoor loves being able to spend his days drawing the animals and pets of his childhood. He especially likes drawing animals with personalities that can be captured in his drawings, such as Latif the lion, Patty the pig, Finlay the frog and Tessie the tortoise.